The Bogey Men and the Trolls Next Door

"Umansky sustains our interest, and a consistently excellent level of writing, right to the poem's fine (and suprising) conclusion."

The Independent

"I read this to 115 Year 5's at an end of term assembly and they were so keen I had to read it twice. Powerful stuff indeed."

Books for Keeps

"Children who like vampires and funny, spooky tales will love it."

Times Educational Supplement

D0635249

The Bogey Men and the Trolls Next Door

KAYE UMANSKY
Illustrated by Keren Ludlow

A Dolphin
Paperback

For James – K.U.
To Tom and Josh – K.L.

First published in Great Britain in 1997
Published in paperback in 1997
by Orion Children's Books
a division of the Orion Publishing Group Ltd
Orion House
5 Upper St Martin's Lane
London WC2H 9EA

This edition published in 2006 for Index Books Ltd

A CIP catalogue record for this book is available
from the British Library

Printed in Great Britain by Clays Ltd, St Ives plc

ISBN 1 85881 244 5 (PB)

Hello! I'm Fred the Bogeyman.

I live beside the bog

With my bogey wife and kiddies

And my faithful bogey dog.

Now, this is Mrs Bogey

In her baggy bogey frock

And her big, black, bogey bovver boots,

Posing by a rock.

(When it comes to breaking rocks up,

Mrs Bogey is the guv.

Her name is really Beryl,

But I always call her "luv".)

Breaking rocks out here on the chain gang...

Here are our bogey children –
Daphne, Bert, and little Douggie . . .

And here is Baby Bogey

In his bogey baby buggy.

And this is Snot, our Bogey dog.

(We've taught him how to beg.)

He eats a lot of Bogey bones

And sometimes bites your leg.

We're a happy little family.

We lead a quiet life,

Just minding our own business

And avoiding stress and strife.

Yes, I'd say we were contented.

Or at least we were before

That very fateful evening

When the Trolls moved in next door!

We were sitting down to supper

With our bowls of bogey stew

(Which is gooey, rather gluey,

And quite difficult to chew) –

When a knock came on our cavern door.

I said, "Who can that be?"

And a voice like grating gravel

Very boomily said **"Me!"**

I opened up the door a crack.

The Trolls stood just outside.

They were rocky. They were cocky.

They were weighty. They were *wide*.

"Hello! We're your new neighbours,"

Boomed the biggest one. **"I'm Dave.**

We've come to introduce ourselves.

We're in the next-door cave."

"This here's my good wife Dolly.
This is Colin, Mol and Polly . . .

"And here's our trollish baby
In her teeny trollish trolley.

"And last, not least, meet Tiddles,
Our charming trollish cat.
I wonder, could we step inside
And have a friendly chat?"

I simply stood and stared at them.

I did not say "How do?"

I did not say, "Do come on in

And have some bogey stew."

I *glared*. I bared my *teeth* at them.

I don't like Trolls one bit,

And wanted to be really sure

They were aware of it.

"I'm sorry," I said coldly,

With my baddest bogey sneer,

"Us Bogeys do not like you Trolls.

We don't want Trolls round here.

"You Trolls make rotten neighbours.

You hold a lot of raves.

You do not bin your rubbish,

You never paint your caves.

"You don't control your children.
You like to scream and fight,
You play loud Trollish music
Very late into the night.

"Well, that is what I've heard, and I'm
Quite sure that it is true."
And I firmly shut the door on them
And went back to my stew.

Well, that was the beginning.

From then on, things went downhill.

Between us and our neighbours

Fell an atmosphere of chill.

And, as the weeks and months went by,
Things slowly got more tense.
The children pulled rude faces
Across the garden fence.

The cat and dog were enemies.

They did a lot of spitting.

The wives were coldly critical
About each other's knitting.

And me and Dave would shake our fists

If ever we should meet

(When we'd been to shop for groceries)

Accidentally, in the street.

The Trolls held noisy parties
And us Bogeys would complain.

But they'd laugh right in our faces
Then they'd do it all again.

They invited their relations
For a sing-song every week,

And bellowed anti-Bogey songs,
Which was an awful cheek.

Their children broke our windows

With their heavy Trollish balls

And at night, they took their hammers out
And hammered on our walls!

BONG! BONG!
BONG! BONG!

Us Bogeys got our own back.

We would sneak on out at dawn

And dump our Bogey rubbish

On their tidy Trollish lawn.

We muddied up their washing

And we trampled on their flowers,

Then acted most indignant
When they came and trampled ours!

We pinched their pints of lava
(We stole them from the crate) –
We wrote anti-Troll graffiti
On their nice new garden gate.

42

We smothered all their doorknobs

With Bogey superglue.

We had to scare them off, you see,

For that's what Bogeys *do*.

We were sitting down to breakfast

Eating Bogey toast and jam,

And our darling Baby Bogey

Was out dozing in his pram.

(We often leave him out there
In the garden, where it's sunny,
Blowing Bogey baby bubbles
And burbling to his bunny.)

"I'll go and check the baby,"
Mrs Bogey firmly said.
"I think he might be sleeping.
I'll just pop him in his bed."

And she strode into the garden.

Then we heard a frightened shout . . .

"Help, everyone! Come quickly!

Baby Bogey has got out!"

It was true. His pram was empty.

What a very nasty shock.

And over by the open gate

(Which we forgot to lock) . . .

We saw little baby footprints
Which we stared at, all agog,
For they led in the direction
Of the dreaded Bogey Bog!

The Bogey Bog! The Bogey Bog!
A place of mud and murk,
All bristling with Danger signs
And snakes, and Things that Lurk.

A stagnant stretch of quagmire,

Very desolate and grim.

No place for Bogey babies

Who have not been taught to swim!

Just then, we heard a startled scream –
And, to our great surprise
The Trolls next door came running out
With wildly rolling eyes.

"Have you Bogies seen our baby?"

Came the chilling Trollish cry,

"Our baby has gone missing!"

"Ours has too!" was our reply.

"They must have gone together,"
Dave the Troll then grimly said.
"We had better go and find them.
Will you come and help me, Fred?"

What a frenzy! What a panic!
We were well and truly worried,
And down towards the dreaded Bog
Us Trolls and Bogies hurried,

And we quite forgot to argue,
And we didn't fight or brawl.
This was a time of crisis –
All for one and one for all!

At last, we reached the Bogey Bog,

Our dreaded destination –

We were worn out to a frazzle

And quite drenched with perspiration . . .

And there we spied our babies

With mud up to their eyes,

Paddling in a puddle,

Busy making muddy pies!

We simply stood and looked at them,
So happy in their game.
Then we looked at one another –
And we hung our heads in shame.

The time had come to call a truce
And try to make amends.
From that moment onwards
We became the best of friends.

Now the children play together
And they have a lot of fun.
The wives sit drinking coffee
In the garden, in the sun.

Dave lends me his mower.

I lend Dave my axe,

And when we meet out shopping,

Well, we clap each other's backs!

The Trolls still hold their parties
And they like to sing at night –
But us Bogeys get invited too,
So that is quite all right.

The fence between our gardens

Fell down the other day –

But we haven't put it up again.

We like the fence that way.

Everything is peaceful now.

No more need for war.

Life is so much better

Since the Trolls moved in next door.